NOT EVERYONE IS NICE

Helping Children Learn Caution With Strangers

By
Frederick Alimonti and Ann Tedesco, Ph.D.

Illustrations by
Erik DePrince and Jessica Volinski

New Horizon Press
Far Hills, New Jersey

For Our Children

Alimonti, Frederick and Tedesco, Ann
    Not Everyone is Nice: Helping Children Learn Caution With Strangers

Cover Design: Norma Ehler Rahn
Interior Design: Susan M. Sanderson

Library of Congress Control Number: 2003100282

ISBN 10: 0-88282-233-0
ISBN 13: 978-0-88282-233-4

New Horizon Press books may be purchased in bulk quantities for educational, business, or sales promotional use. For information please write to New Horizon Press, Special Sales Department, P.O. Box 669, Far Hills, NJ 07931 or call 800-533-7978.

www.newhorizonpressbooks.com

SMALL HORIZONS
A Division of New Horizon Press

2010   2009   2008   2007   2006   /   6   5   4   3   2

Printed in Hong Kong

My name is Kathy.

I live with my mom and dad and my little brother, Eric. He is only two years old.

We also have a cat. His name is Spoons. We gave him that name, because he has a black spot on his back shaped just like a spoon.

I am in kindergarten. My teacher's name is Mrs. Roberts. She is very nice. She reads us stories and teaches us about all sorts of things like science and nature. She also lets us bring in things to share with the class on Show-and-Tell days.

Some days, my mommy picks me up from school. Other days, I go home with Grandma and sometimes I go home with a friend. I wait on the corner right near the crossing guard for my ride home.

I always know in the morning who is coming to get me at the end of the school day. Mommy and Daddy always tell me never to go home with anyone else or to get into a car with someone who does not have permission from them to take me home.

The person who is going to pick me up sometimes is a little late. When that happens, I'm supposed to wait by the door of the school. If the person doesn't come soon, I am supposed to go back inside the school and tell my teacher that my ride did not come. This only happens when my mommy has to work late or there is a mixup. I play in my classroom until Mommy comes to get me.

One day, I was waiting by the curb for my mom to pick me up after school. She was late. I was about to go to inside the school to wait when a car stopped in front of me. The man inside the car rolled down the window.

The man driving the car was wearing a funny, green wool hat with a pom-pom on top. He also had on a matching green sweater. He looked like he was a nice person.

"Is everything okay?" he asked. "You look lonely or lost."

"I am not lost or lonely," I told him. "I am just waiting for my mommy to come get me and take me home."

"Where do you live?" the nice man asked.

"On Grant Street," I told him.

"That is funny," he laughed. "I live on Grant Street, too."

I didn't think it was very funny, but he smiled and laughed, so I laughed, too.

"What is your name?" the man asked me.

"My name is Kathy," I said.

"Hi, Kathy. You can call me Mr. Green," he said politely.

"I am going home right now. Why don't you hop in and I'll give you a ride home, too. I bet you know the way. You seem very smart," he said with a smile.

"I can't ride with you, Mr. Green. My mommy told me to wait here for her."

"I would be happy to bring you home to your mommy. She is probably worried about you. Maybe she is late, because she is hurt or sick and could not come to get you. We should hurry," he said.

I was worried now. Maybe Mr. Green was right. Maybe Mommy was hurt or sick.

"Look," Mr. Green said. "I have some chocolate. I bought it for my little girl. She is about the same age as you. You can have some if you promise not to tell her. Her name is Lisa. Do you know her?"

"No, I don't know anyone named Lisa."

The man reached out the window to hand me a small chocolate bar.

I leaned forward to take the candy bar, but before I could get it, I felt a hand on my shoulder pulling me back. I turned around. It was Mommy. She looked very upset.

"Who are you?" she asked the man.

"That's Mr. Green, Mommy," I said.

The man did not say anything. He just drove away very fast. The chocolate bar fell to the ground.

I was very sad. "Why did the nice man drive away so fast?" I asked.

"He was not a nice man, Kathy," my mom said. She promised we would talk about him later at home.

Mommy drove us to the police station. We went to the front desk and Mommy spoke to the policeman on duty. She said she wanted to report a stranger who talked to her daughter. The policeman wrote a lot of stuff down and then told my mom they would look into it, whatever that means.

When she was finished talking with the policeman, Mommy gave me a big hug and we went home.

Later that night, after my brother, Eric, was asleep (I get to stay up later because I am bigger), Mom and Dad came into my room. Daddy had a big book about the ocean with him. It was very colorful and had lots of pretty pictures of the sea and different kinds of fish.

"Mommy told me about the man in the car today," Daddy said. "We both want to talk to you about what happened. Mommy said you thought the man in the car was very nice."

I nodded. "Yes, he had a funny hat and a chocolate bar and a little girl the same age as me."

"Kathy," my dad said, "sometimes things and people are very different from what they seem. Some people aren't nice at all. Even though they may seem nice, they can hurt you."

"I don't understand," I said.

"Maybe this book will help you understand," Daddy said. He opened the book to a picture of a yellow and red underwater plant. You could tell it was underwater, because there were fish swimming around it.

"What a pretty plant," I said.

Daddy shook his head. "It's not a plant," he explained. "It's an animal called a sea anemone. It fools fish by looking like a plant so that they won't be afraid to come near it. Then, when the fish get close, the sea anemone eats them for dinner!"

"Oh no! Really?"

"Yes," Daddy said, "it gobbles them right up."

Mommy took the book and turned to another picture. It showed a beautiful fish with orange and white stripes and big fins swirling all around its head like a lion's mane.

"It looks like an animal from the jungle," I said laughing.

"That's right," Mommy said and smiled. "It is called a lion fish, because it looks a little like a lion and because it can be ferocious and dangerous. You see, this fish's pretty fins are full of poison. If another fish gets too close, it gets stung and then the lion fish gobbles up the other fish for dinner."

"That is amazing," I said. "I guess you shouldn't pet it."

"That's for sure," Mommy said, nodding.

"Kathy," my dad said, "even in nature, you cannot tell if something is safe just by how it looks. The same is true for people. Some people may look very nice and act kindly, but that may be to fool you; some of them can hurt you."

"Like the sea anemone fools the fish?"

"Yes, just like that," my dad said.

My mom said, "People may seem nice or look handsome or pretty, but they can be dangerous like the lion fish. So you have to be very careful. Strangers may seem nice or say nice things, but they may not be nice people. You should only go places and accept gifts from people you know very well, like your family, your close friends and your teacher."

"Remember, Kathy," my dad said, "you can never be sure if a person is really nice just by looking at him or talking to him."

"What should I do if I meet another stranger who seems really nice, like the man in the car?" I asked.

"Well, Kathy," my dad said, "if a stranger tries to get you to go somewhere with him, just quickly walk away and ask a grown-up you know for help."

"Like my teacher?"

"Yes, Kathy, that's a great idea. The grown-up will know what to do and will be able to tell if the stranger is nice or is really a 'lion fish' in disguise!"

I never saw the man in the car again. If I do see him again or if someone else I don't know tries to take me places or give me things, I will remember what my mom and dad told me about the sea anemone and the lion fish. I will walk away and ask a grown-up I know for help.

It makes me a little sad that not everyone is nice, but I do know lots of people who are really nice and that makes me feel happy.

— The End —

TIPS FOR KIDS

1. When you go places or play outside, go with friends, not by yourself; it is safer.

2. Before going out, always tell a parent or person in charge where you are going, who will be with you and when you will be home.

3. If no one is home and you must leave, always leave a note about where you will be and a phone number.

4. Tell a parent, teacher or counselor if someone makes you uncomfortable or afraid.

5. Don't get into a car with a stranger or even with someone you do know when you do not have your parents' permission. Walk away.

6. Don't let anyone touch you or treat you in ways that make you scared or uncomfortable.

7. Do not accept gifts, even small things like candy, from anyone without a parent or trusted adult there to say it's okay.

8. Practice things you should do in case of an emergency, like calling 911.

9. Don't be polite to a stranger if you feel you are in danger. Make noise and try to run away.

10. Go to security or the police if you get lost or separated from your parent while at a shopping mall or other public place.

TIPS FOR PARENTS AND GUARDIANS

1. Set up rules about where and with whom children can go places. Always know where your children are.

2. Teach children to be wary of strangers and to follow their instincts if they are uncomfortable or afraid of people, even relatives.

3. Teach kids to say "No!" and get away from scary people and situations.

4. Teach children to immediately check with a caregiver if an unfamiliar adult approaches them.

5. Play "what if" games with your children so they will know what to do if strangers approach them with typical ploys such as "I'm looking for my puppy" or "I need directions."

6. Teach children to dial 911 and be sure they know their addresses and phone numbers.

7. Do not leave young children alone.

8. Create a secret password in case someone other than a family member has to pick up your child.

9. Teach children to go to security or the police if they are lost or get separated from you in public places.

10. Carry a recent picture of the child with height, weight and other important identifying information on the back.